BEE WALSH

An imprint of Enslow Publishing

WEST **44** BOOKS™

Please visit our website, www.west44books.com.
For a free color catalog of all our high-quality books,
call toll free 1-800-542-2595 or fax 1-877-542-2596.

Cataloging-in-Publication Data

Names: Walsh, Bee.
Title: Manning up / Bee Walsh.
Description: New York : West 44, 2020. | Series: West 44 YA verse
Identifiers: ISBN 9781538382677 (pbk.) | ISBN 9781538382684
  (library bound) | ISBN 9781538383346 (ebook)
Subjects: LCSH: Children's poetry, American. | Children's poetry,
  English. | English poetry.
Classification: LCC PS586.3 W374 2020 |
  DDC 811'.60809282--dc23

First Edition

Published in 2020 by
Enslow Publishing LLC
101 West 23rd Street, Suite #240
New York, NY 10011

Editor: Caitie McAneney
Designer: Seth Hughes

Photo credits: cover (helmet) studiogstock/iStock/Thinkstock;
cover (texture) -slav-/iStock/Thinkstock.

Printed in the United States of America

CPSIA compliance information: Batch #CS18W44: For further information contact
Enslow Publishing LLC, New York, New York at 1-800-542-2595.

*To all the men and boys who have been told to "man up"
and are still angry about it. This is for you.*

COACH SAYS

Coach says

I need to keep
my head down
when I rush
the defensive end.

Running back.
Head down.
Eyes up.
Take him
down.

Coach says

I need to lift
my feet.

Coach says

I need to focus.

Coach says

I have to be
ready for Friday.

I have to be
ready.

1

EYES ON THE PRIZE

Today at practice,
Coach asks me
where I see myself
in five years.

Five years.

"Here, I guess."

"No son,
where do you want
to be?"

"Here, I guess."

"Jack,
you need to get
your eyes on the prize."

The prize.

What is
the prize?

ANYTHING

I'd give anything
to be able
to put on
invisible clothes
like that wizard kid
in that book.

Walk around
and no one
would look
at me.

No one
would pat me
on the shoulder

and ask me
about the game.

No one
would ask me
how my mother

is holding up.

I could do
anything
and no one
would say anything
about it.

MOM

Mom had me
when she was
my age
now.

Seventeen.

She had Beth
two years later.

She said
from the moment
she met
our dad
when she was 12

in the same town
we live in now

that she was
gonna love him
for the rest
of her life.

When Dad died
eight years after
I was born,

I heard Mom cry
and make sounds
I didn't know
people could make.

Beth and I don't
talk about it
but I hope
every day
that she doesn't
remember.

But it never
stopped Mom
from putting
dinner on the table.
Or putting
herself through
night school
to become
a paralegal.

These days,
she helps people
who are here illegally
figure out
their rights
and how
they're gonna
feed their kids,
too.

IT'S HARD

It's hard
growing up
in the same town
that your
parents did,
and their parents
before them.

Everyone
knows
everything
about you.

Texas
is funny like that.

Everyone knows
if you miss
church on Sunday.

Everyone remembers
your father's funeral.

It's hard, sometimes,
when everyone
wants you to
"go on to better things"
and all you
want to do
is stay.

FIRST

I was one
of the first
guys in my
grade

whose voice
got deeper
and face
got hairy.

I was taller
than everyone
my age
by the
eighth grade.

And running
sprints
on the field
with the
varsity team
when I should
have been
with JV.

MAKE IT

All the guys
say I
"make it look easy."

Me and the QB
throwing
the ball
halfway
across the field.

Easy isn't
getting up early
every morning
to run five miles.

Easy isn't
three times a day
in the weight room.

Easy isn't
hating myself
every night
at dinner

because
I don't want
Mom or Beth
to worry
about why
I don't eat.

SOMETIMES

I can't even
believe that
Beth and I
are related.

She amazes me
with all the crap
she gets into.

Last year,
she decided
she wanted
to be one of
those people
who build houses
or schools
or something.

Now,
she makes me
drive her
all over the place,
wearing her
bright blue shirt,
hammer in hand.

When she was 10,
she told Mom
and me
at Christmas
she wanted
to be a doctor
"just like Dad."

And that's
when I knew
she didn't remember
him at all.

REST IN PEACE

You know how
sometimes
after someone has died,
you sort of
fill in the details
of their life
to make their story
better?

I think that's what
Mom did after
Dad died.

Sort of told us
the stories
as she wanted to
remember them.

Not that Dad wasn't
a really good man,
just that he didn't
live long enough
to have that many
stories to tell.

Mom would tell us
about their first
date,
how he swept her
off her feet.
Or how much
he loved helping
his patients.

In reality,
Dad dated Mom's
best friend
for a year
before they started dating.
And he wasn't
a doctor—
he did billing
for a local
doctor's office.
And fixed cars
on the weekend.

I like the stories
that Mom tells us.
So I don't correct her
when she fills
in the details.

THROUGH THE WALLS

When I was nine,
I heard Mom crying
in her bedroom
through the wall
of the room
I shared with Beth.

We were supposed
to be getting our
own rooms.
But after Dad died,
it was like
everything
in the house
froze.

I know
that she cried
often
because I would
wake up early
and see
her red face.

But that night
I heard her,
and all I wanted
was for Beth
not to wake up.

I think I
grew up
that night.

I never
wanted to
make
Mom cry
like that.

And I never
wanted Beth
to know
anyone
could ever
be that sad.

SEVENTEEN YEARS

I don't know
if any 17-
year-old guy
is

      normal.

Or maybe there
is no such thing.

But whatever it is,
it can't feel like this.

Or at least

everyone else
doesn't look like
they feel this way.

LITERALLY

I literally
cannot stay awake
during chemistry.

It's not like
I'm not good
at it.

I study. I get A's
and sometimes
B's.

But I just don't care
about negatively
charged ions.

I just want
to get onto
the field
and run.

I need to feel
my body under
my pads
under
the sun.

Where nothing
can touch me.

TOWNS LIKE THESE

Comfort, Texas.

They make
TV shows
about towns
like mine.

Fourth-generation
families.
The men
still wearing
their championship
football rings.

Girls pushing
strollers down
the same streets
their moms
pushed them down.

The whole town
closes down
and crams into
the bleachers
at the high school
on Friday nights
to watch the
Comfort Bobcats.

The same way
we all
pack into
the pews
of the churches.

I think most guys
my age
either can't wait
to get out
and not be like
their parents.

Or they will propose
to their probably
already pregnant
girlfriends
at prom
and buy the house
next to
their parents.

I think that
I'm somewhere
in the middle.

I wouldn't
have chosen this town,
but I don't hate it
now that I'm here.

THE NOTE

Someone put
a note in my locker
before homeroom.

The handwriting
looked kinda like
Beth's or Mom's,
but there were
hearts over the i's.

The writer
said they were
looking forward
to watching me play
Friday night
against our rivals.

They said they'd be
holding a sign
with my number on it—

19.

They said
I should keep
an eye out for them
rooting for me.

GIRLS

I am too nervous
to look for a girl
holding a sign
with my number.

Instead,
I take down
every guy
who gets in my way
and we
crush
the other team
until we win.

I can't talk
to girls.

Not girls
who hold signs.

Not girls who leave notes.

Not girls
who want to talk to me.

MOM ASKS

Mom never asks me
directly
if I'm dating anyone.

But she always finds
ways
to almost ask if
I'm dating anyone.

"Do you have any *special* plans
this weekend?

"The cheerleaders
really seem to be
fans
of yours."

"I saw in the paper
the movie theater
downtown
is offering
two-for-one deals on
Sunday evening
tickets,
if you're interested."

I hate brushing her off,
but I hate even more
that she has to ask
at all.

ANOTHER NOTE

This morning,
I find another note
slipped inside
my locker
on game day.

> "I'll be holding up
> your sign
> again."

> "I like that
> your hair
> falls in your face
> when you
> walk
> down the halls."

I shove the note
in the back
of my locker

and go
to math class.

HEAVY

It's too

heavy

most days.

Carrying around this weight.

Carrying around this body.

Trying to do
the best.

Trying to be
the best.

Too heavy.

NO FEELING

There's
no feeling
like rushing
40 yards

through a crowd
of men

thinking
they can stop me.

Right
to that
touchdown
line.

They
can't
stop
me.

HARDER

At practice,
Coach yells
while we run

that the harder
we train,

the harder our
opponents
will fall.

The harder
we train,

the harder our
opponents

will

fall.

AT NIGHT

Some nights,
I stay up
late

after Beth
and Mom
have gone
to bed.

Looking
at pictures
of pro
football
players
online.

Their bodies
and their
game
are so
controlled,

so disciplined,

and it shows.

I think that
I could never
be that strong,
that fast,
or that
good.

I stay up late
at night
and look up

      meal plans

and

         gym plans

and
try
to be

         good
         enough.

BURGER AND FRIES

It's tradition

to go out
after each game
to Waring's General Store.

All the guys
on the team,

the cheerleaders,

fans,

moms and dads.

Waring's serves
the best burger,
fries,
milkshakes
in town.

The sesame buns,

the buckets of
ice cream,

the glass
Coke bottles.

It hasn't changed
in 50 years,

kinda like this town.

The guys all order
burgers
and milkshakes.

Their girls
pick fries
off their plates.

I've found
that if I don't
sit down
at any one table
for too long

no one questions
why I don't

order anything.

TIRED

This week
I have been
so tired

that even
Coach
noticed.

> "What's wrong
> with you, *boy*?"

I don't say
that I haven't eaten
in three days.

I don't say
that I'm not sleeping.

I don't say
I don't know
if I even want
to go
to college.

> "Just a little
> under the weather,
> sir."

DAD'S

There's a picture
on the fireplace
at home.

Dad sitting
in the front seat
of his
1986 Chevrolet K-20
pickup.

> "One of
> the only
> brand-new things
> your dad
> ever owned,"

> Mom says.

> "That truck,
> you,
> and your sister."

He loved
all three
just the same.

When I was
old enough
to drive,

I went down
to the used car lot
in town
and told Bill

I wanted a
1986 Chevrolet K-20.

Just like Dad's.

It took seven months,
but we finally
tracked one down.

It needed
a new transmission.

I didn't care.

A year after I turned 16,
I finally had
my truck.

Just like the picture
on the mantel.

TERRY

I've known Terry,
well,
almost my whole
darn life.

Terry's mom died
when he was born
and Terry's dad
hasn't been the same
since.

Mom jokes
that Terry
is her third kid

because of how often
Terry
has eaten dinner
with us

and how many
of Terry's pictures
went up
on our fridge
when we were
kids.

He's like
a little brother
to me.

I keep eyes
on him
when he gets
into trouble
at school.

And I think
I'm the only
reason that
Coach let him
on the team.

Terry's always scribbling
in that notebook
of his.

And I'm always,
well,
doing what I do.

> Brothers
> have secrets, too,

> I guess.

DREAM

It's always
the same dream
before a big game.

Dad, Mom, and Beth
cheering
from the sidelines.

And me

100 miles away
trying to get there,

unable to find
my way.

MORNING

No one likes
early practices
that Coach
insists
are the

difference

between
good teams
and

great ones.

BEST DAYS

My best days
are the ones
when I know
everyone
has
everything
that they need
from
me.

When Mom
doesn't
stay up late
at
the kitchen table
looking
at bills.

And Beth
doesn't cry herself
to sleep
because kids
are real mean.

And we've won
another game
and the guys
punch me
in the arm
in celebration.

The best days
are the ones
I don't have
to think about
anything
at all.

NO

Coffee.
Cigarettes.
Alcohol.
Drugs.
Junk.
Snacks.

MIRROR

I spend
too long
looking
in the mirror
at my body.

I look at
the muscles,
the bruises,
the fat,
the hair.

And I wonder
why I care
so much.

And if
the other guys
look at
their bodies
as much
as I do.

CHOKING

When we go out
to dinner,

Mom, Beth, and me,

I can't not order food.

Every bite
feels like I'm choking,

like it's going to come
back up.

Sometimes I think
they notice.

Sometimes I think
Mom looks sad.

Like she knows
something,

but isn't sure
what.

INTERRUPTED

I have study hall
every other day
during fourth period.

I study during
study hall,

which the guys
used to
pick on me for.

They stopped
after I got
a 3.5 GPA
junior year.

Today,
while I was
doing my
AP U.S. History
homework,

my guidance counselor
came into the library
and interrupted me.

Asked if I could
come with her
to her office
for a few minutes.

I had only been
to her office
a few times before.

Choosing classes.
Once after I got
into a fight.

She wanted
to talk to me
about
"how I was doing"
and
"if I felt ready."

Ready for what?
I wasn't sure
at first.

"Ready
for the rest
of your life?"

I shrugged.
But I didn't answer.

I didn't know
how to tell her

I wasn't.

FOMO

I can't
imagine
leaving home
for good.

Once a month,
Beth, Mom,
and I

make pizzas
and watch
a movie.

It's my job
to go to
the store
on the way home
from school

so Mom doesn't have to.

Beth likes to spend
too long
picking out
toppings.

I like
to let her.

I don't want
to miss out
on movie nights

or any other
nights

away from
them.

EVERY TIME

I start to think
about high school
ending,

and how
everything
is going to change,

I feel like
I'm going to barf.

Most days,
I am sick
to my stomach.

So sick
I can't eat.

So sick
I don't want
to eat
for days.

THE HALLWAYS

Every day
it's the same.

Same classrooms,
same posters,
same hallways.

Same conversation
with Mom
over my cereal.

Same ride to
school with Beth.

Same locker-room
talk with Terry.

"Excited for the
game this week,
honey?"

"How many times
have I told you
not to touch
my radio, nerd?"

"Dang, boy,
where you find
them muscles?"

Same worry
about
letting them all
down.

PUSH HEAVY

I read this line
in this
small book
my sister left
in the kitchen.

It said
to "push heavy."

Something about
fireworks.

Something about
fighting the
Big Sad.

I didn't understand
a lot of what
was in the book.

But I understand
being sad.

And I understand
pushing heavy things.

And I understand
how heavy
sad
can be.

BE THE MAN

At the dinner table.
On the field.
In the weight room.
For my sister.
For my mom.

HOME TO MOM

This is how
it's always been,
after school, after practice,
after hanging
with the guys.

I'm the one

who kills the spiders.

And I'm the one

who double-checks
the doors are locked
at night.

I come home
to Mom
and to Beth,
no matter what.

That's how it's
always been.

I CAN'T

I never say it
out loud.

Not to Mom,
        not to Beth,
                not to Coach,
                        not to anyone.

I can't.

I can't eat pizza
with the guys.

I can't let them
watch me

chew,

and chew,

and chew,

and not swallow.

I can't waste
the food Mom
works so hard
to get for us.

But I can't wait
for her
to go to sleep
so I can throw it up.

I can't tell Coach
why I'm so tired
when he needs me
not to be.

And I can't give
excuses to the guys
on the line
when I miss
the block.

I can't be less
than they need
me to be

and I can't be more
than I can stand.

NOT MUCH

There's not much
I know
that feels like
getting in front of the guy

trying to get in front
of our quarterback

seconds before
the whistle blows.

There's not much
I know
that feels like
knowing I'm the fastest guy
out there.

Not much like
pushing down
five guys

and still
standing.

225 DAYS

Some of the kids
already have
countdowns
in their lockers.

It's only September!

Only 225 days left
until we're
out of here.

Only 225 days left
until we're
out on our own.

I don't have
a countdown
in my locker.

I'm not ready
for all of this
to be over.

BETH ON THE WEEKENDS

Beth always asks
for rides to school,
like I'm going to say,
"No."

She makes me take
her in early
so she can tutor
the middle schoolers
in math or
biology.

I have to wait for her
to finish her
Honors Club meeting
after practice.
Fifteen minutes
always turns to 30,
but I don't mind.

Because Beth
on the weekends
wants to go to
the movies
with Mom and me,
wants to
go grocery shopping
instead of partying.

Beth wants to watch
a movie with me
on a Saturday night,
when maybe I'm not
feeling quite myself.

I don't mind waiting
15 minutes
for Beth
to get out of her
nerd club
because we won't have
these drives home
for much longer.

I love Beth,
especially on
the weekends.

THE LETTER

I come home
to Mom crying
in the kitchen
today.

Mom is holding
a letter
in one hand
and covering
her mouth
with the other.

I think maybe
it's something
about the house
or
Dad's pension.

Instead,
she hands it to me
to read.

"Congratulations, Jack,
on being accepted to…"

It's not about
the house
or money.

It's about me,
and how someone
at a college

wants to pay me

to come play football

for them.

Mom isn't
crying
because she's
sad
or scared.
She's crying
because she's
not
anymore.

HANDSHAKES

When I walk
into the locker room
after school today,
Coach looks me
straight in the eye
and reaches out
his hand
for mine.

So does
the offensive coordinator
and the defensive coordinator
and the quarterback
and everyone
on the line.

They all shake my hand
and say that
I deserve it
and that
they are proud
to play with me.

Who will I be
when I am
no longer
in this locker room
with these guys
to shake my hand?

ON THE WALL

When I get home
from practice
today,

I see
that Mom
has framed
my acceptance
letter

and hung it
on the wall

next to our
baby photos.

She put a
bow on it,

like it is
a gift.

I don't know
if it is

to me

or

from me.

STUDYING

I thought
maybe
that after
I was accepted
into college
I wouldn't
have to study
so much.

But now I feel
like there's
even more
pressure
than
before.

Like
now that
I have it,
I could easily
lose it.

Like if I work
harder
and run
faster,
I can't
let them down
farther.

So I take
all the books
home from
my locker
every day.

And run
five more
sprints
than Coach
says I have to.

I can't lose it
now that
I have it.

SATURDAY NIGHTS

All the guys
go out
with their girls
on Saturday nights,
like it's just
that easy.

They go to
the movies
to make out

or the hills
to make out

or the fields
to make out.

I take Beth
to the diner
to get her
a milkshake,
or stay home
and watch
game film.

I've never had
a girl
to take out
on a Saturday night.

I don't know
how
to ask them

or why
they would
want to.

THE GYM

I was getting
out of the shower
at the gym
after lifting
yesterday
when I saw
one of the trainers
come in
and drop off
a small plastic bag
to someone else's
locker.

Like he was
hoping
no one
would see.

It didn't
take me long
to realize
what it was
when
the biggest
guy in the gym
came in and
took his stuff
out of
that locker.

THE TRAINER

Ever since
I saw that trainer
drop something
in the big guy's locker,

I've been wondering
about how much
bigger
I could get

if I talked
to that trainer.

ASKING

When I woke up
this morning,
I barely knew
how to find
the words
I would need
to ask
for a small
plastic bag.

But by late afternoon,
I had found them.

And by evening,
I had used them.

PLASTIC BAG

After I got
out of the shower
from lifting,
I found
a plastic bag
in my locker,

containing
a few bottles,
needles,
and instructions.

I quickly
stuffed them
in my gym bag

and hopped
in my truck
to speed home.

NEEDLES

I didn't mind
going to the doctor
when I was a kid.

Shots didn't bother me.
I knew
it wouldn't hurt
that bad.

And I saw
how stressed
my mother got
when my sister
cried and cried
about them.

So why is it
that now
as I sit in my bathroom
in the middle of the night

holding a needle
full of
anabolic
steroids,

my hand shakes?

EFFECTS

I wondered
if I would
actually
notice
the effects

after I
finally
got the needle
into my skin.

But at practice

I timed my

full field sprint
down two seconds.

> "I've been training
> hard for you,
> Coach."

I say,
as I feel my heart
pound
in my chest.

WORSE

I know
I should feel
worse.
I should feel bad.

But man,
these days,

I am feeling good.

Faster.
Stronger.
Fitter.

I am

waiting

for the shoe
to drop

or whatever
they say.

NUMBER 19

I get another
note today.

Just my number
drawn on an
index card

stuffed into
my locker.

This time,
I don't
crumple it up
and toss it.

This time,
I shove it
in my pocket
for later.

RITUALS

Some of
the guys
are really
funny before
a game.

They do
a certain number
of pull-ups

or say
a Hail Mary.

I shake hands
with Coach
on the way
to the field.

We all do
what we need
to win
the game.

LOOKING UP

I pull
the index card
with my number
on it

out of my gym
bag and put it
in the weight
room locker.

I've decided
that after the snap,
I'm going
to look up
into the stands

for a girl

holding a sign

with my number

on it.

So,

I do.

A GAME LIKE THAT

I haven't played
a game like that

maybe ever.

Maybe it's
because
playoffs are
coming up.

Or maybe it's
because
someone
other than
Mom and Beth
was in the stands
for me.

Someone with long,
brown, curly hair.

But the other team
didn't score
a single touchdown

and we were like
gods.

200 DAYS

Halfway
through the
season,

and I feel
like a different
guy
than when it started.

Everyone said
senior year
wouldn't be
like the rest
of high school.

And maybe
I didn't believe them.

And maybe
I wanted them
to be wrong.

And maybe
I will
be okay.

WARING'S GENERAL STORE

Everyone is
saying that I
am the reason
we dominated
the game
tonight.

Everyone wants
to pay for
my food
and smack
my shoulder
and shake
my hand.

Coach
is seated
on the other
side of Waring's
with his wife
and little girl.

He's looking
at me in a way
like he's
not really sure
what he's
looking at.

He's looking
at me like
he's seen
young men
like me
before.

He's looking
at me
like
he knows.

ANOTHER ONE

I find
another note
in my locker.

This one asks
if I had
thought about
if I might
go to the
Homecoming Dance
or not.

Honestly, I
hadn't.

Obviously,
I'll play
in the Homecoming
Game

and go to
the pep rally.
Mostly because
Coach says
we have to.

The dance.
Huh.

She says
I should
let her know
by scoring
the winning
touchdown
on Friday.

I want to say
that's not really
what running backs
do,
but I've
never actually
said anything
to her
at all
before.

I'VE BEEN THINKING

Laying in
bed,
staying up
too late
last night,

that maybe,
it wouldn't be
the worst thing
to go
to Homecoming.

What am I
saying?

What do I
know about
dances?

Or girls?

FIRST TIME

For the first time
in a long time,
I ask Mom
for advice
when she
gets home
from work.

HOLE IN THE WALL

I never used
to understand
people who
let their
emotions
control them.

That never
used to be
who I was.

Now I feel
like I've got
a hair trigger.

One thing
goes wrong,
and I want
to put my fist
through the wall.

I yelled at Beth
because she
used all the
hot water
when I just
wanted to take
a shower
after practice.

When was
the last time
I yelled at Beth?

When was
the last time
I was so angry
I could hit
something?

ALL NIGHT

I stay up
all night,
reading the
side effects
of steroid use
online.

You hear about
all the bad stuff
that will happen
to your body,
but you hear
about it in
after-school
TV specials
and movies
about athletes
who rose and fell.

You don't think
about sitting
in the same
pink tile bathroom
your mom used
to bathe you
and your sister in,
filling a needle
and jamming
it into your thigh.

You don't think
that you're going
to break out
on your face
and back.

You don't think
you're going to
bruise from every hit.

You don't think
your blood pressure
will rise so high
you can feel it
in your teeth.

But it all seems
worth it
when you're
flying down the
field
to score
the winning
touchdown.

ALMOST

Coach is
mad something
fierce today.

Says we've been
unfocused this week.

Says he doesn't
know what our
problem is.

When Coach
is mad,
we run.

And run.

And run.

And we run
up and down
that field
so many times,
I almost
pass out

for the first time
since I first
picked up a
football.

And it is in that
moment

when I fall to
my knees
and catch
Coach's eye,

that I know
that he knows.

PAYING FOR IT

Ever since
practice last week
when I fell
on the field,
Coach has been
riding me.

He doesn't know
what,
but he knows
something.

He's been
keeping me longer
and pushing me
harder.

Like if he
can just get
me to crack,
he can figure out
what's going on.

But Coach
doesn't understand
how badly
I need this.

I need this.

PLAYOFFS

We have
a chance
this year
to go
all the way.

Coach
has been
at this
high school
for his whole
life.

He used to rush
dudes
on this very
field.

His senior
year
was the last time
that this
school saw
a championship
at States.

And now
here we are,

20 years
later,
and I think,
we're not just
doing this
for our own
rings,

but for Coach
to win
as well.

BILLS

Mom seems
so much lighter
ever since
the letter
from the university
arrived
in the mail.

She has always
wanted more
for Beth
and me
than to stay
in this town
and relive
the same lives
as everyone.

Beth and I
are the reason
she works
all that overtime
and stays up late.
Bills all over
the dining room table.

I can hear her
talking to Dad,
and she sighs
into the checkbook.

So, when we found out
that some people
wanted to pay
for me to go
to school,

I could see
the look in her eyes
that it was all
worth it.

So, how could
I possibly think
of ever

ever

letting her down?

THE WEIGHT

Everyone wants
to look like the
people they see
on TV and in
the movies.

All those muscles,
that good skin,
that good hair.
We don't want
to think about
how many hours
those people
spend at the gym.
Or stand in front
of the mirror
in their house,
hating themselves.

I do.
I think about it.

I spend hours in
the weight room
before and after
school,
lifting,
pulling,
heaving,
counting down
the calories
from the day.

I think about
the weight of
my body.

The weight of
taking us
to playoffs.

The weight of
not letting
Mom and Beth
down.

The weight of
keeping all
these secrets.

QUALIFIED

Not in
20 years
has our
little town
of Comfort

gotten this
close to
going to
States.

But last night,
when we broke
the two-and-a-half-
quarter-long tie

with the winning
touchdown
in the last
second,

it was like
you could hear
the town
wake up.

THE TOUCHDOWN

I hadn't decided
when we went
onto the field
last night

if I was the
type of guy
a girl would
want

to go to
Homecoming with
or not.

All I've ever
wanted is for
no one to
ever look at me.

And now
I can't stop
thinking about
the girl

with the brown
curls in front
of her face

and how
she looks
at me
from the stands.

I want to yell,

"DON'T LOOK
AT ME."

But also,

"Please,
see me."

HOMECOMING

It's not until
it's already
happening
that I decide
I am going to do it.

Nine seconds left
on the clock
and I see QB
pass me on
my left and I
know where
we're going.

In that moment,
I want
to be seen.

In that moment,
I know
there isn't anyone
getting in our way
as we take
everyone down
who tries to stop us.

In that moment,
I take off for
the end zone

with the ball midair
like I was born
to catch it.

And catch it,
I do.

We win
the game.
But all I can
think about
is the girl
with the brown
curls
falling
in her face.

QUIET

When I look up
from the end zone
as the final whistle blows,

I should see
Coach throwing
his hat into the air.

Or the team
all running toward
me and QB.

Or the stands
full of everyone
from town
rushing onto
the field.

But the only
thing I see
is a girl
standing
in the bleachers
holding a sign—

19.

And it all
goes quiet.

HELLO

After the game
that ensures
the Comfort Bobcats
are going to playoffs
for the first time
in 20 years,

I'm not sure
what is making
my heart pound more.

The adrenaline?

The injections?

The girl?

Before I can
take a breath,
Coach shouts
for us to line up
to shake the hands
of the other team.

We have to push
our way through
the crowds
of fans on the field.

And for a moment,
I think I see
her brush past me.

But when I turn my head,
she is gone.

After the handshakes,
we rally our way
into the locker room.

Coach gives us
the kind of speech
you hear in movies
about high school football.

I don't hear
a word
of it.

I don't hear
a word
of anything.

Until I get
to my truck
and see the girl
with brown curls
leaning on the hood.

"Hello."

HELLO, PT. 2

It's like
the whole world
goes from
mute

to the volume
all the way up.

"*Hi.*"

"How does it feel
to have scored
the touchdown
that will take y'all
to playoffs?"

And that's when I
all of a sudden
feel my heart
pounding
in my
entire body.

Like I need
to sit down
right now
or I might
pass out.

And somehow
she knows that,
even though I don't
say anything.

> "Why don't you
> sit down before
> it all catches up
> with you?"

I don't want
to think about
everything
catching up
with me.

I can't stand
the thought.

MISSED OUT

I've never
not gone out
with the team
after a game
Friday night.

Until I find
myself and Ellie
sitting in my truck
behind the field house
at the high school
for hours
after the game.

I learn
Ellie moved to
Comfort
two years ago
from Oregon
because her dad
is in the Air Force.

I learn it's the
12th time she's moved
in her life.

I learn her
younger sister
is friends with
my younger sister.

And I learn
that she decided
to leave a note
in my locker
after she saw me
defend a freshman
in the cafeteria
when he was
getting picked on
for dropping
his tray.

Also, she tells me
she's borrowing
a green dress
from her mom
to wear to
Homecoming.
And she doesn't
like cut flowers,
so I don't have to
buy a corsage.

Whatever that is.

WEDNESDAY WITH TERRY

"Do you even
know how to
talk to a girl,
man?"

Terry says as
he shovels
Mom's fried chicken
into his mouth.

He's come over
after we spent the
afternoon trying
to get his
1955 Pontiac Chieftain
to finally
start.

"I don't know
about talking,
but I did
a good amount
of listening,"

I say as I push
the chicken
closer to him.

"You sure
she knew
it was your locker
when she
dropped
the note in?"

I laugh and
roll my eyes.

"She knew
at least
it wasn't yours."

GROCERY SHOPPING

Every time
we win a game,
I feel like
I get taller,

but not
in a good way.

The taller
I get,
the more
everyone
notices me
whenever I'm
around.

Yesterday,
Mom asked me
to pick up
breadcrumbs
at Lowe's Market.

What should
have taken me
10 minutes
ended up
taking me
almost an hour.

Everyone wants
to stop
and talk to me
about how
they think
I should
play the game.

I can't even
make it from
the door
to my car
without Mr. Sheel
telling me
to keep
my shoulders down.

I think the
only thing
I am
looking forward to
after graduation

is that I won't be
this tall
anymore.

THE COUNTDOWN

Part of me thinks
I don't know
how we got
this far,
farther than
we've ever
gotten before.

Playoffs.

But the other part
of me knows
we got this far
because we
really
worked for it.

The things
that I have done
in the past
two months.

Man,
I don't even know
who I'm going
to be when
this is all over.

Will I be
the guy
who makes
his mother
proud?

Or will I be
the guy
who
can't even
look her
in the eyes?

NEW SUIT

Mom looks
at me
with her
squinted eyes
and small smile
when I tell her
I'm going
to the Homecoming
Dance.

Like she wants
to be really careful
of what she says next,
or I might
run away
and slam
my door.

After about
half a minute,
she asks me
if I want
to buy
a new suit.

Nah.

GETTING READY

I stand
in front
of the bathroom
mirror,

trying to convince
myself to
get into
the shower.

I can't stop
looking
at my shoulders.
Acne I've
never had before.

Stretch marks
on my sides,
strange hairs
on my chest.

I can't breathe.

I turn the shower
as hot as it gets
and stand under it
until I want
to pass out.

Doesn't it say
somewhere in
the Bible
that you need
to be made pure
with fire?

I turn the water off
and sit down
in the tub,
using every muscle
in my body
to keep my eyes
from filling with
tears.

What girl
would want
a guy
as weak
and awful
as me?

But it's too late
now to not go.
That's not the son
my dad would
have wanted.
Or the one
my mom raised.

Out of the shower
and into
my old suit,
a new green tie

to match Ellie's dress.
My shaking hands
can barely knot it.

Mom, knocking
on my bedroom door,
wants a picture
before I leave.

Wants to know
if I want to
take her car
instead of
the truck.

Wants to know
when we can have
Ellie
over for dinner.

My shaking hands
cover my mouth
to keep
from throwing up.

On the way
to my truck,
I can hear
Coach's motto
in my ears:

> *"ALWAYS EARNED,*
> *NEVER GIVEN."*

YES, SIR

I haven't even
thought about
having to meet
Ellie's
parents before
I pull up
in front of
her
house.

Her Air Force father
answers the door,
and I freeze
for a moment
before reaching out
to shake his hand.

> "You must be
> Jack?"

> "Yes,
> sir."

> "C'mon in."

Ellie
is standing
in the entrance
to the living room
in a dress

the color of
a ring
my grandmother
used to wear.

Emerald,
I think.

Her mother
stands between us,
camera in hand,
doing something
with her smile
that is half joy
and half fear.

(Later,
Ellie
will tell me
that I am the first
guy she's ever
brought home.)

"You played
a good game Friday.
That was quite
the final touchdown."

"Yes,
sir."

After pictures,
and a short,
quiet lecture from
Ellie's
father that
reminded me
of something
I might hear
from Coach,
we get into
my truck and
leave for the dance.

It isn't
until after a
few minutes of driving
that I realize I have
gone silent.

"You don't seem
like you've done
this before."

"Which part?"

Which is when
Ellie
laughs in a way
that makes the
bottom of my
stomach drop out,

but in a good way.

1000 THINGS

Mom always listens
to this old musician
from the early 2000s
named Jason Mraz.

He's got this song
that she plays all
the time
when she's missing Dad
called
"1000 Things."

I had never
understood
what Mraz meant
when he said
that he'd seen a
thousand things in one place,
but then stopped counting
when he saw her face.

Until I saw
Ellie laughing
with a group
of her friends.
And I felt like
I wanted
to keep her
laughing
like that
forever.

I walked over
to her and put
my arm around
her shoulders
and felt her
wrap her arm
around my waist.

In that moment,
something changed.
We weren't just
two kids
at a dance.

We were in it
together now.

SLOW DANCE

Whoever had
the job to hang
fancy lights
and shiny ribbon
from the ceiling
knew what they
were doing.

I almost forgot
we are in the
same gym
I have P.E. in.

And when the DJ
changes the music
from some pop song
to something slow,
all I want to do
is pull Ellie close.

I don't care
who is watching.

I don't care
about anything
except for
my arm around
Ellie's waist.

SATURDAY MORNING

The morning after
the Homecoming Dance,
I have to take
my truck down
to the shop
for a new belt.

Jeff gives me a
discount on parts
because I do
the work myself.

When I am
pulling into
the parking lot,
I notice an
envelope tucked
into the
passenger side
visor.

As I take
it down and
hold it in
my hand,
I think about
Ellie
sipping on fruit punch
and smiling
as Coach, QB, and I

listen to everyone
tell us their own
story about
the last time
Comfort
went to playoffs.

I think about
how dry my mouth
would get every time
she
asked me a question.

And how it took me
until the last slow song
to get up the courage
to ask
her
to dance.

I open the note,
chuckle,
and stuff
it in
my back pocket.

They say that
a girl always
remembers
the first time
she slow dances
with a boy.

You can add
last night
to a long list
of reasons
I'm going to
remember you
for the rest
of my life.

x,
E

ALWAYS EARNED

Ever since
we made playoffs,
Coach has been
running us ragged.

"ALWAYS
EARNED,
NEVER
GIVEN,"

we yell as we
run suicides.

I can feel my
body burning
as the air
struggles to
get to my blood.

I am the best
and worst
I have ever been.

But I can't think
about that now.

I am running
toward
my future,
whatever that
may be.

NEVER GIVEN

When I wake up
the morning of
the first playoff game,
I feel like
all of Earth's gravity
is pulling my limbs
to the ground
and I can't get up.

Beth knocks on my door,
telling me we're going
to be late if I don't
get my butt in gear.

I have a pain
in my chest,
like gravity is
squeezing my lungs.

In the truck
with Beth,
she asks me
about
Ellie.

I tell her that
Coach hasn't
given us
any time off
since Homecoming.

She clicks her tongue
at me.

"Knock it off,
Beth. I don't have
time to worry about
anything but
football right now."

As soon as
the words come
out of my mouth,
I know I've
hurt her feelings.

She slinks down
in the seat
and stays quiet
until we get
to school.
Slams the door
when she gets out.

Same pain
in my chest.

GAME TIME

There's a sort of
calm that comes
over me in the
moments leading
up to a game.

I don't have any
rituals like some
of the guys do.

I don't need to
listen to a
certain song.

I don't need to
say a prayer
a certain number
of times.

I just get
quiet.

Quieter
than usual.

Quiet enough
to hear Coach
enter the locker room
and say,

"Gentlemen,
how do you
want to be
remembered?"

And I think
to myself,

Not like this.

GOING DOWN

A football game
is like a dance.

Planned.

Coach can see
where we are
going before
we get there.

Usually, I just
drown out the
crowds and my
thoughts.

Focus on
just being
on the field.

But all I can
see is
the letter on the wall.

Beth in my truck.

Mom at work.
Ellie in the stands.
Coach on the sidelines.
Dad when I was a kid.

And I feel the
pain in my chest
again.

But this time
it is more
of a throbbing.

I can hear
QB calling
the final play
of the game:

A Swinging Gate.

If we can
complete this
surprise, we will
win the game.

The offensive line,
but no center,
lines up to one side of the field.

QB and I
on the other.

All I have to do
is make a short run
and score the touchdown.

That's when it
all goes
black.

SLOW MOTION

In the seconds
between when

I catch the pass
from the QB

and take off
running

to the end zone,
I feel every

single muscle
in my entire

body stop.
Like someone

has turned off
all the lights

in the house
at once.

As every light
goes dark...

I THINK ABOUT

losing my scholarship,

losing my family,

losing myself.

And I can't
do anything

but lay down
in the dark.

THE TRUTH

I wake up
in the hospital
a day later.

They tell me
I had a
cardiac episode.

Which means
that basically,
my heart stopped.

When I open
my eyes,
I see Mom
sleeping in a
chair next to
my bed.

And my sister
curled up
next to me.

They had both
been crying.

HOURS LATER

I tell
them
everything.

I tell them
about the steroids.

I say
"I'm sorry"
more times
than I
can count.

I say
that it wasn't
anyone's fault
but my own
over
and
over.

I say
that I
was scared.

Of letting down
Mom.

Of letting down
Dad.

Of failing.
Of losing
my scholarship.

Of leaving.
Of staying.

Of being
a man.

DYSMORPHIC BODY

The doctors help
me find the words
for everything
that I've been
holding in,
for the first time
in my life.

I learn to say
"body dysmorphia"
and
"disordered eating."

Apparently,
1 in 50 people
have body dysmorphia.

That's a lot
of people.

People who
have it
spend way more time
than people
who don't
thinking about
what parts of
their body
make them
unhappy.

Hours a day.

Maybe even
all day.

And no matter
what anyone tells them
about that part
of their body,
they only see
what they don't like.

WEEK THREE

I've been in
the hospital
just under
three weeks.
They have a
rehab here.

Every day,
I've met with
doctors,
counselors,
therapists.
All these people
who want
to help me
get better
and
go home.

At first,
it was really
hard to tell
all these
people
I don't know
from nothing
all the secrets
I've been keeping
for years.

But once
I got started,
I couldn't stop.

It was like
seeing the
goalpost
get closer
yard by yard.

They say
that I'll get out
in a few days.

I still have
a lot of work
to do.

STATES

Well,
they made it.

We made it?

We won
the playoff game
that almost
killed me.

And they won
the next
three games
after that.

And we made it
to the State
Championship.

And I won't
be playing in it.

VISITORS

When I got out
of the cardiac ICU
and entered rehab,
they let me
have visitors
other than
Mom and Beth.

Terry was
the first
to come by.
Then QB
and the rest
of the team.

Everyone says
the same things:

> "You gave us
> a good scare
> out there!"

or

> "Just glad to see
> you're alright."

I can tell
that everyone
is a little
uncomfortable
standing at
my bedside,
like they don't
know what else
to say.

I'm just glad
they came
at all.

That I didn't
let them
down.

TICKETS

Coach comes by
with an envelope
to give to me.

It has three tickets
to the big State game,
and a pass for me
to ride with the team.

Coach is a man
of few words,
pursed lips,
and a
firm handshake.

He wants me
to know that
even with
everything that
happened,

everything
that I did,

he is still
proud of me.

He says he hopes
I don't make
another mistake
like this again,

and that I will be
on the sideline
with my team
as we win States.

ON THE FIELD

It's a four-and-a-half-hour drive
from Comfort to Arlington,
just outside of Plano, Texas.

I'd only ever been
all the way up here once,
before they tore
the old stadium down.

We are all
pretty rowdy on the bus
for most of the drive,
but things quiet down
as we get close.

We have to check in
first.
But I didn't
expect to
have to go through
the locker rooms
and across the field
to get there.

I DON'T KNOW

if I've ever felt
as big
and as small
at the same time
as I do right now,
standing
on this field.

THE BIG GAME

I thought that
I knew how loud
a stadium
full of people
could be.

But I had no idea.

From the moment
the game starts,
it's like
there is some sort
of electricity
or something
just everywhere.

Everyone is
moving just
a little bit faster
and hitting just
a little bit harder,
even our rivals.

We are neck and neck
every minute of the game.
Every time they score,
we do, too.

They pass block
deep, and we
push back strong.

I honestly don't think
any of us know
who is going
to win.

And it isn't until
the final seconds
on the clock,
as our guys
race to intercept
a pass going to
the end zone,
that we know.

Because we catch it
and win.

FREEZE

We have won
games before,
obviously.

But as the
final second
ticks away

and the scoreboard
reads 53-49,

it's like
all the sound
in the world
drops out.

There is
a moment,
before we all run
to the field

and the crowd
goes wild,
where time
freezes.

Like we all
get an extra second
to experience

the greatest moment
of our lives.

And then all the sound
comes rushing back.

ALMOST

I want nothing more
than to be happy for
my team
with my whole body.

But there is a big
part of me that thinks
that if I hadn't been
so weak, so stupid,
then I would have
been playing
in the big game, too.

I try as hard
as I possibly can
to get these thoughts
out of my head.

It's hard to combat
a lifetime of
hating yourself
with a few weeks
of therapy.

A LETTER

The therapist
from the rehab

says that I
should try
writing a letter
to my dad
to tell him
how I feel.

Which doesn't
make a lick
of sense to me
because he
can't read it.

She says
that it doesn't
need to
make sense
in order
for it
to help.

DEAR DAD

It's been
almost 10 years
since you died.

I was just
a kid back then,
and I guess
that I'm
a man now.

For a long time,
I was pretty mad
that you left.

But the more
I got
to know you
through Mom,
and stories,
and pictures,

the more I
realized that
you would never
have left us
if you had
the choice.

Everything
that I've done
and everything
that I am
is because
of you.

I wanted
to grow up
to be
the kind of
man
you would
be proud of.

Smart.
Strong.
Good.

And somewhere
along the way,
I think
I lost myself.

Mom says
that she gets
to join you
way before
I do.

So from here
on out,
I'm going
to try
to do right
by me
to do right
by you.

I miss you,
Dad.

I hope
that you're
happy
wherever
you are.

Love,
Jack

COACH'S OFFICE

School's out
for the holidays,
but Coach calls
and asks me
to come see him.

I've never before
been nervous
to go into
Coach's office.

He tells me
to have a seat,
that we need
to talk.

I'm thinking
that he is
going to tell me
that they pulled
my scholarship.

Which would be
terrible,
and awful,
but not the end
of the world.

Instead,
he tells me
I will still
be going to
college in the fall,
fully funded.

It's like
I can't
understand
the words
as they are
coming out
of his mouth.

Coach tells me
that I shouldn't
be punished
for making
a mistake
when all I
wanted to do
was the right thing.

Coach says
that everything
that happened
will stay
between us,
and no one else
needs to be
involved.

All the university
required was for
the doctor to
tell them
I was healthy
enough to play.

And that will
be that.

LAST NIGHT

Last night,
Beth came into
my room
and sat on
the end of my bed
like she's done
a million times
before.

But this time,
she didn't seem
to know
what to say
to me.

I could tell
she was trying
to make up
her mind
between
yelling
and
crying.

Instead,
I pulled her
in close
and hugged her
hard
for a while.

All she said was,

"Don't scare me
like that
again."

"I won't."

"Promise?"

"Promise."

WHAT I LEARNED

In therapy,
I learn that
what I have
is technically called
"muscle dysmorphia."

This includes:
obsessing about
being muscular,
spending many hours
at the gym,
abnormal eating patterns,
and use of steroids.

I learn that the more
research
is done on guys,
the more they
realize that

almost as many
males have
body dysmorphia
as females.

I learn that
I may never be
"cured,"
but I certainly
will be
better.

But that
it's going to
take work.

       "I'm not afraid
       of hard work,"

I tell my
therapist.

       "You should see
       me and QB
       rush a 40-yard pass.
       Now, that's work."

I go to a support
group of guys
with eating disorders
every week
in San Antonio.

Beth drives
with me
every Saturday,
45 minutes
each way,
and sits in
the waiting room.

She says
there's
nothing else
she'd rather
be doing.

Through all
of this,
the thing that
I learn
the most about

is how much
the people
who love you
want to help you
get better.

ELLIE

After the holidays,
I get in the car
on a Sunday morning,
and drive over
to Ellie's house.

I haven't talked
to her since the
day I collapsed.

I don't know
if she'll be mad
or what.

But I know
I owe her
an apology, too.

Her mom answers
the door and
smiles at me.

I ask if I could speak to
Ellie for a few minutes.

"We prayed for you
every week at church,"
her mom says.

Ellie comes to
the door, asks her
Mom for some
privacy, and shuts
the door behind her.

We sit on the
front porch swing
in silence
for a few minutes.

When I'm done
telling Ellie about
the steroids,
the anger,
passing out,
the hospital,
and therapy,
she looks at me
good and hard
and rests her head
on my shoulder.

I don't know
if it is the smell
of her hair
or the warmth
of her hand in mine,

but I pull her chin
toward me
and kiss her.

FIRST KISS

Most guys
wouldn't want
to admit
that they had
their first kiss
at 17.

I think
the guy that
I was
a year ago
didn't think
about it at all.

But now,
well, now
I can't stop
thinking
about it.

And when
I can kiss her
again.

SAY IT

My therapist
makes me
repeat after her
for five minutes
every session.

It's like a game
only I can win.

> "I am
> good enough."

> "I am
> good."

> "I am
> enough."

> "Say it,"
> she says.

And I do.

I am good.
And I am
enough.

And I can finally
say it.

80 DAYS

Today,
Terry tells me
that there are just
80 school days
left of
senior year.

I don't know how
that could
possibly be.

There are still
classes,
finals,
prom,
nights out.

I think that before,
I didn't want to
think about
it all ending.

But now
I can't stop myself
from thinking
about it all
beginning.

USED TO BE

I used to be
so afraid
of leaving home,
of leaving mom
and Beth.

I used to be
afraid
of weakness,
of letting
everyone down.

But now I have plans.
Plans for
the future.

Plans to
attend college,
maybe major
in social studies.

Plans to
visit Ellie
on the weekends
at Baylor.

Plans to
call Mom
at least
once a week.

I no longer
feel like
I'm going
to fail
at everything
I touch.

It's like
I can see
a future now

when before
all I saw
was fear.

PRACTICE

I have to practice
looking into the mirror
at myself.

I'm supposed to
say, or at least think,
things that I like
about myself.

My therapist
explained it as
conditioning,
which made sense
to me.

You have to
do something
over and over again
until you're
really good at it.

Like going to
the weight room
or running the field.
I stand in front
of the mirror
every morning
and smile.

SINCE STATES

Ever since States,
there's been a
kind of life
in Comfort
that I've never
seen before.

Every shop
has a big ole sign
hanging in its
window.

People stop
us on the street
to shake our hands.

I hear the principal
telling Coach
that there might be
some money
to fix up the field
for next year.

I think that
winning States
was the best thing
we could have done
for our hometown.

I still can't
figure out
what the opposite
of "letting someone down"
is, but whatever it is,
that's what we did.

We'll always have that.

DINNER TABLE

Tonight,
Mom, Beth and I
are eating dinner,
a rare night without
Terry.

And Mom gets up from the table
and goes to the hall closet.

She brings back
a small package
that I didn't see
come in the mail.

I can tell
that her and Beth
are real excited
by the way they
look at me.

Mom puts it down
next to my plate
for me to open.

Mom and Beth
bought me a T-shirt
from the school
I'm going to.

The school that is
only two hours away,
but where everything
will be different.

PROM

If you had asked me
two years ago,
or even a year ago,
if I thought that
I would ever
be going to prom,
let alone with a date,
I would have
pretended I didn't hear you.

But here I am,
wearing a suit and a flower,
standing in Ellie's
living room, waiting
for her to come down.

And when Ellie,
in her purple dress
like the color
of the sky
right before
the sun sets,

comes down
the stairs
before we go
out to my truck,
she stops to
look at me. Says,

"This is going
to be a good night,
I can tell."

I don't know
how she knows that
or why she is
so sure,

but I do know
I want
to find out.

SUMMER

Summertime
in Texas
just sort of
arrives one morning.

All of a sudden,
we all go out
to our cars and trucks
and the steering wheels
are too hot
to touch.

My whole life,
the start of summer
has meant the start
of hot months
running the field,
conditioning
in the stuffy
weight room,
and driving Beth
to whatever
new volunteer
or church thing
she signed up for.

This time,
my hot truck seats
mean something new
is about to begin.

BREAKFAST

Ever since
I got out of
the hospital,
Mom has been
making breakfast
every morning
for all three of us.

She does it half
because the doctors
told her that
food needed to be
something celebrated
and shared.

Half because
I think she's also
starting to realize
that I'll be leaving
soon.

Most mornings,
it's oatmeal
or eggs,
sometimes pancakes.

Every morning,
she asks Beth and me
what our plans
for the day are
and what we want
for dinner.

Every time,
there's a moment
right before
we clear our plates
that Mom pauses,
looks at us both,
and smiles.

I'm gonna miss
these mornings,
but I'm gonna
take them with me.

And I know
that Mom and Beth
will be okay
when I leave.

GRADUATION ROBE

This morning,
all the seniors
go to the cafeteria
to pick up
their graduation robes.

We ordered them
at the start of
the school year.

Back before
the steroids,
the hospital,
the State game.

Before Ellie.

The person
picking up
the robe
is a totally different
person than
the person
who ordered it.

The person
picking up
the robe
can look
himself,
his mother,
his sister,
his girlfriend,
his coach
in the eye
and feel good
about what
they see in him.

The person
picking up
the robe
can leave
and not worry
about who
he's letting down.

The person
picking up
the robe
is no longer
controlled by
his eating disorder.

He's in control,
and ready for
whatever comes
next.

LAST DINNER

It's tradition for
the Boosters to take
the football team
out for dinner
at the end
of every school year.

To say goodbye
to the outgoing seniors
and welcome
the incoming newbies.

This will be
the fourth dinner
that I've gone to.

But this will be
the first dinner
where I actually eat.

And the first dinner
Coach's speech
will be directed at me
and QB.

This dinner
is gonna mean
something to me
for so many reasons.

GRADUATION MORNING

I can't believe
that I almost
didn't make it
to graduation.

That I hated myself
so much
I almost
took myself away
from the people
who love me.

But here I am
on a hot and sticky
Texas morning
in May.

Wearing a black
graduation robe
and the same shoes
I wore to Homecoming
and prom.

Trying to remember
which side
my tassel goes on.

I feel really excited
and really normal
at the same time.

Mom won't stop
crying, and Beth
won't stop trying
to fix my tie.

We all wish
that Dad
was here, too.

I just want
to stay awake
through the
whole ceremony.

The football
seniors stayed out
pretty late last night.

One last hurrah
before we all go
our separate ways.

I can't believe
I almost
didn't make it.

ORANGE AND WHITE

My first game
wearing orange
and white.

The crowd is
100,000 people
to Comfort's
1,500.

Mom, Beth,
and Ellie
in the stands.

Every part
of my body
hurts in the
best way possible
after more intense
conditioning
than I've ever done.

I still can't
believe they
chose me.

But let's never
say that
hard work
doesn't pay off.

Because as
we run onto
the field, I feel
every feeling that
I've ever felt
in my whole life
at the same time.

And it feels
amazing.

WANT TO KEEP READING?

If you liked this book, check out another book
from West 44 Books:

I AM WATER
BY MEG SPECKSGOOR

ISBN: 9781538382790

The Thing About Rivers

They have
a way
of f l o w i n g
through you
when
you've worked
on one
long enough.

Guide a river
for
a few years
and
it ends up
guiding
you.

Check out more books at:
www.west44books.com

ABOUT THE AUTHOR

Bee Walsh is a poet, freelance editor, and introvert from the Bronx, NY. She attended SUNY Fredonia and received a degree in English language and literature, as well as international studies. She has been published in such literary journals as *Velvet Tail, Vagabond Lit,* and *Wyvern Lit,* as well as *Synaesthesia Magazine,* where she is currently the poetry editor. Walsh wanted to write a book about something she understands very well (eating disorders) and something she knew little about (football). You can find her at beewalsh.com.